Tadpoles
Nursery Rhymes

Baa, Baa Black Sheep

and

Baa, Baa Pink Sheep

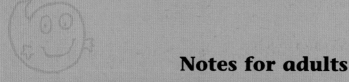

Notes for adults

TADPOLES NURSERY RHYMES are structured to provide support for newly independent readers. The books may also be used by adults for sharing with young children.

The language of nursery rhymes is often already familiar to an emergent reader, so the opportunity to see these rhymes in print gives a highly supportive early reading experience. The alternative rhymes extend this reading experience further, and encourage children to play with language and try out their own rhymes.

If you are reading this book with a child, here are a few suggestions:

1. Make reading fun! Choose a time to read when you and the child are relaxed and have time to share the story.

2. Recite the nursery rhyme together before you start reading. What might the alternative rhyme be about? Why might the child like it?

3. Encourage the child to reread the rhyme, and to retell it in their own words, using the illustrations to remind them what has happened.

4. Point out together the rhyming words when the whole rhymes are repeated on pages 12 and 22 (developing phonological awareness will help with decoding language) and encourage the child to make up their own alternative rhymes.

5. Give praise! Remember that small mistakes need not always be corrected.

First published in 2008 by
Franklin Watts
338 Euston Road
London NW1 3BH

Franklin Watts Australia
Level 17/207 Kent Street
Sydney NSW 2000

Text (Baa, Baa, Pink Sheep)
© Mick Gowar 2008
Illustration © O'Kif 2008

The rights of Mick Gowar to be identified as the author of Baa, Baa, Pink Sheep and O'Kif as the illustrator of this Work have been asserted in accordance with the Copyright, Designs and Patents Act, 1988.

ISBN 978 0 7496 8022 0 (hbk)
ISBN 978 0 7496 8029 9 (pbk)

Series Editor: Jackie Hamley
Series Advisor: Dr Hilary Minns
Series Designer: Peter Scoulding

The author and publisher would like to thank Frances Gowar for permission to reproduce the photograph on p. 14.

Printed in China

Franklin Watts is a division of Hachette Children's Books an Hachette Livre UK company.
www.hachettelivre.co.uk

Baa, Baa, Black Sheep

Retold by Mick Gowar
Illustrated by O'Kif

FRANKLIN WATTS
LONDON • SYDNEY

O'Kif

"I remember when my children were very little. I read them rhymes or counted sheep until they went to sleep. Although, sometimes, I fell asleep first!"

Baa, baa, black sheep,
have you any wool?

Yes sir, yes sir,
three bags full.

One for the master,

and one for the dame.

One for the little boy
who lives down the lane.

Baa, Baa, Black Sheep

Baa, baa, black sheep,
have you any wool?
Yes sir, yes sir,
three bags full.

One for the master,
and one for the dame.
One for the little boy
who lives down the lane.

Can you point to the
rhyming words?

Baa, Baa, Pink Sheep

by Mick Gowar
Illustrated by O'Kif

Mick Gowar

"This is me in my shed. This is where I write my books. When I'm not writing I like visiting schools to read my books and tell stories to the children."

Baa, baa, pink sheep,
have you any wool?

No sir, no sir,
none at all.

17

None for the master,

and none for the dame.

None for the little boy who shivers down the lane.

Baa, Baa, Pink Sheep

Baa, baa, pink sheep,
have you any wool?
No sir, no sir,
none at all.

None for the master,
and none for the dame.
None for the little boy
who shivers down the lane.

Can you point to the
rhyming words?

Puzzle Time!

Can you spot which of these are made of wool?

Answers

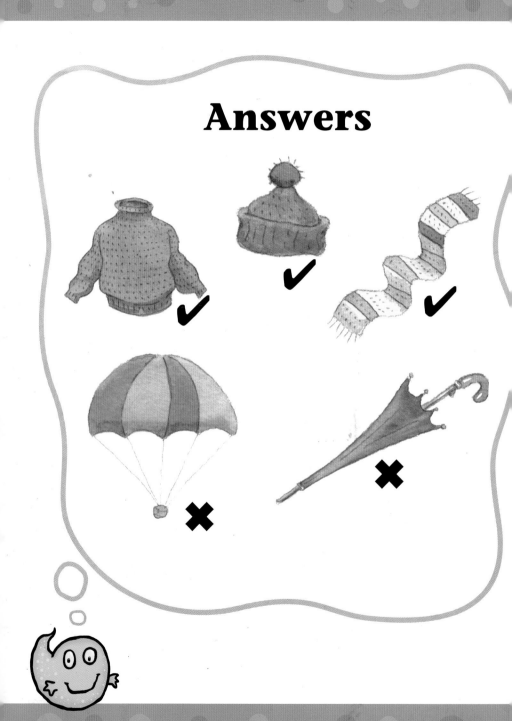